Calming Colouring
patterns

BATSFORD

First published in the United Kingdom in 2014 by
Batsford
1 Gower Street
London
WC1E 6HD

An imprint of Pavilion Books Group Ltd

ISBN: 9781849942690

A CIP catalogue record for this book is available from the
British Library.

20 19 18 17 16 15
10 9 8 7 6 5 4 3 2

Repro by Mission Productions Ltd, Hong Kong
Printed by 1010 Printing International Ltd, China

This book can be ordered direct from the publisher at the website:
www.pavilionbooks.com, or try your local bookshop.

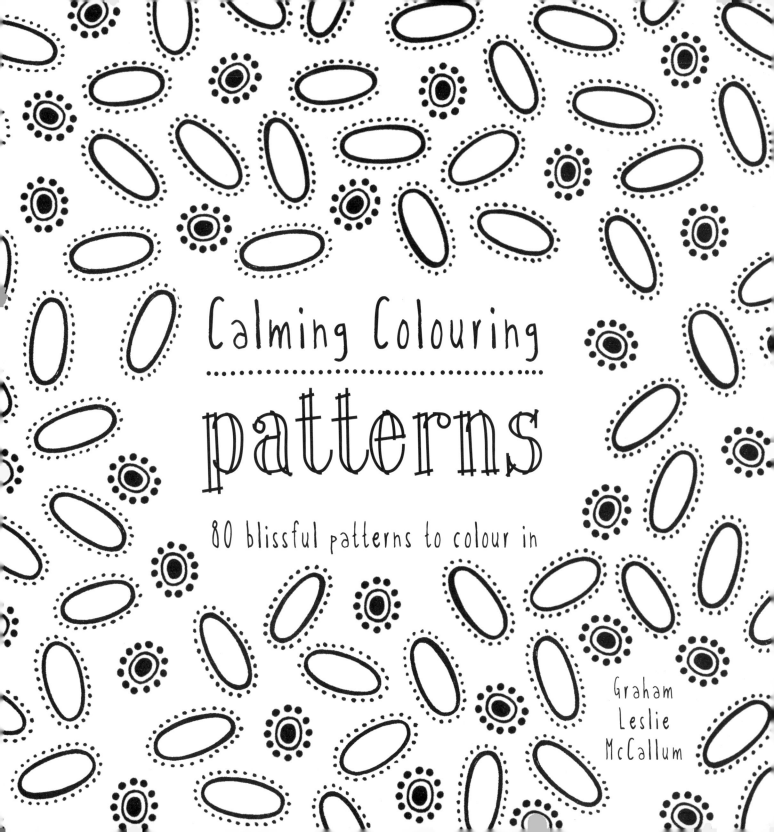

Calming Colouring

patterns

80 blissful patterns to colour in

Graham
Leslie
McCallum

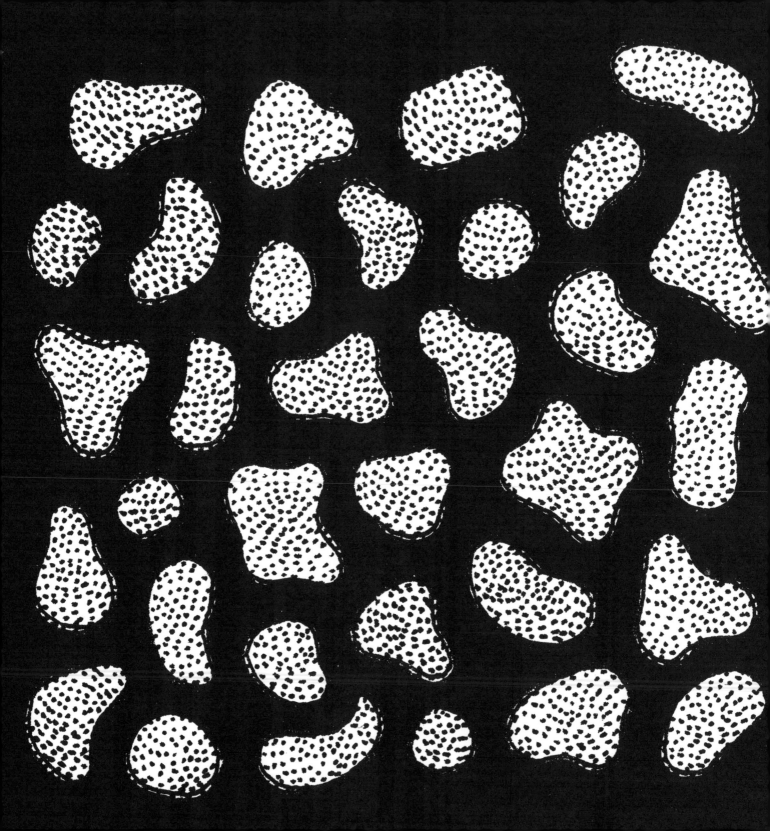

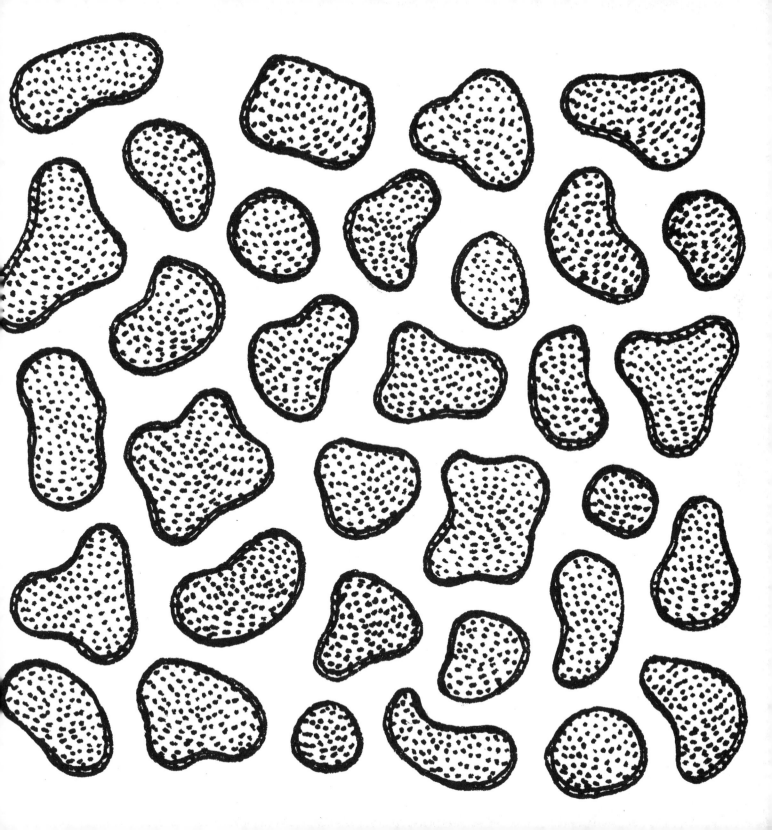

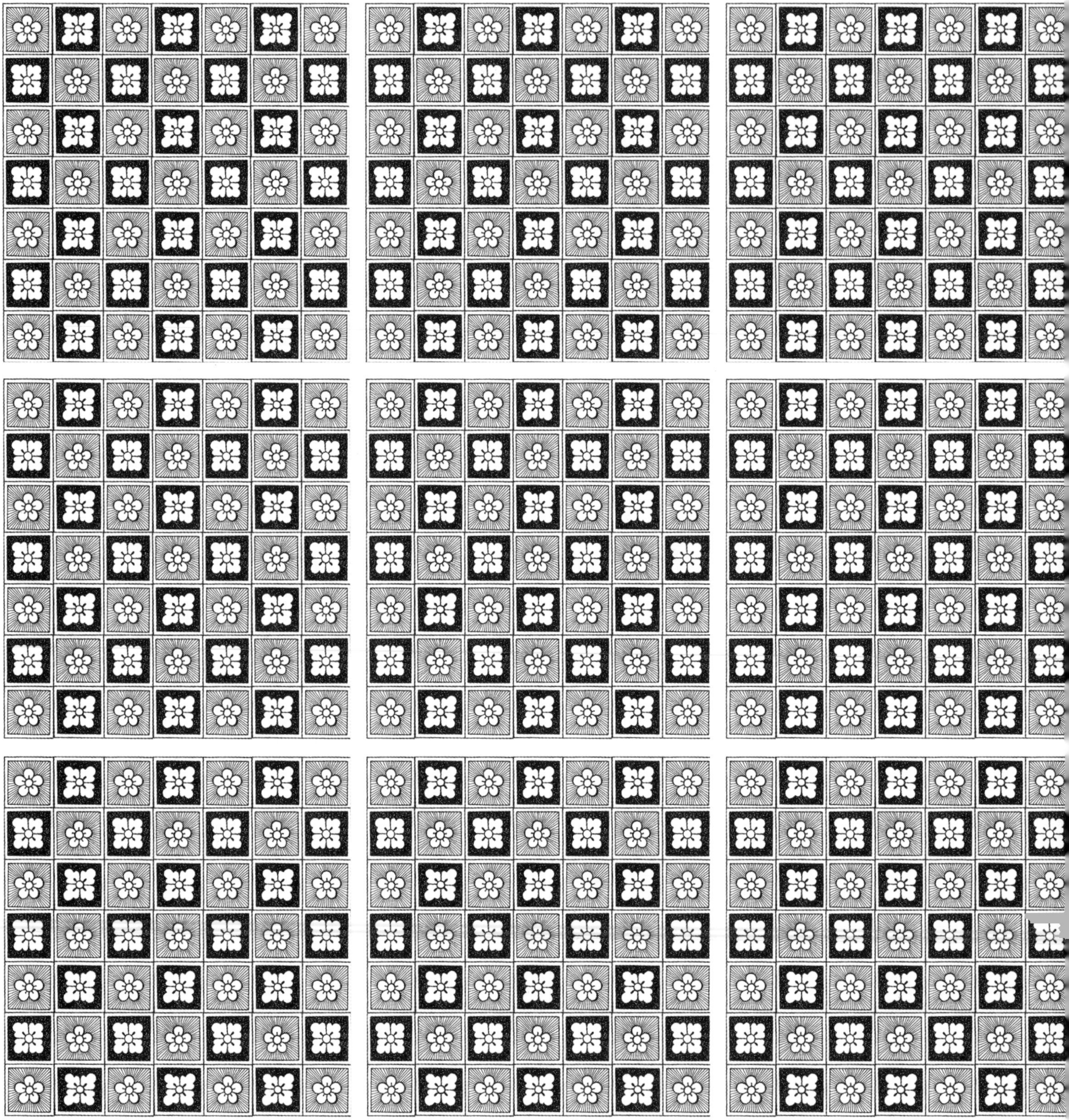

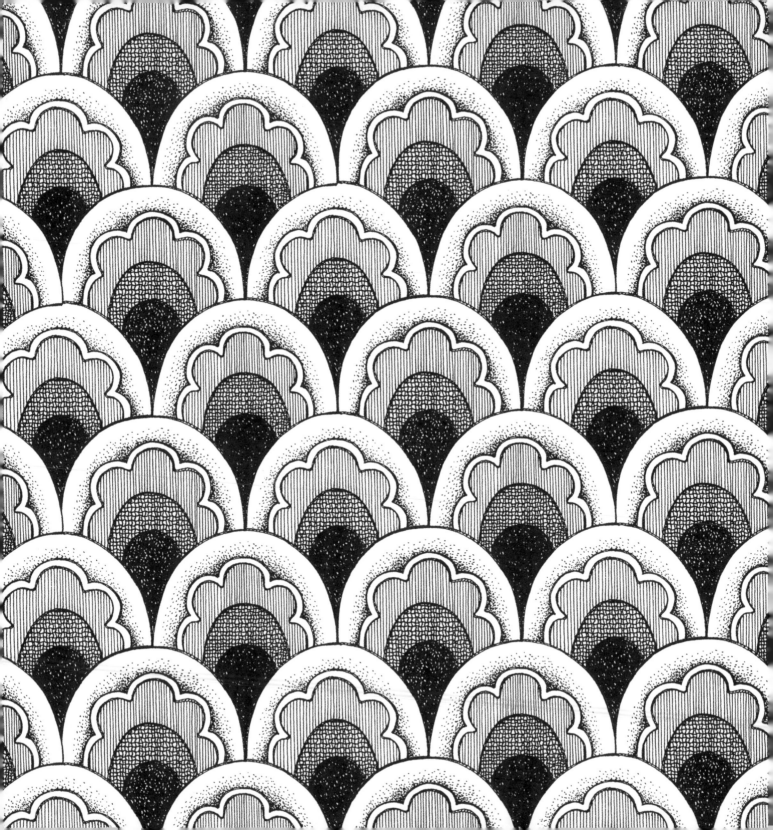

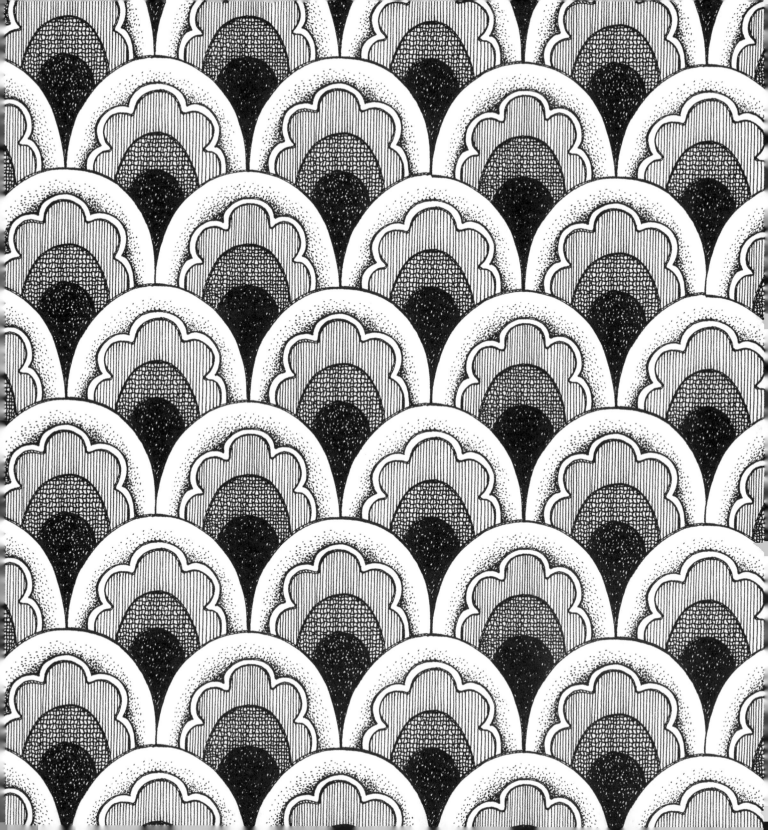

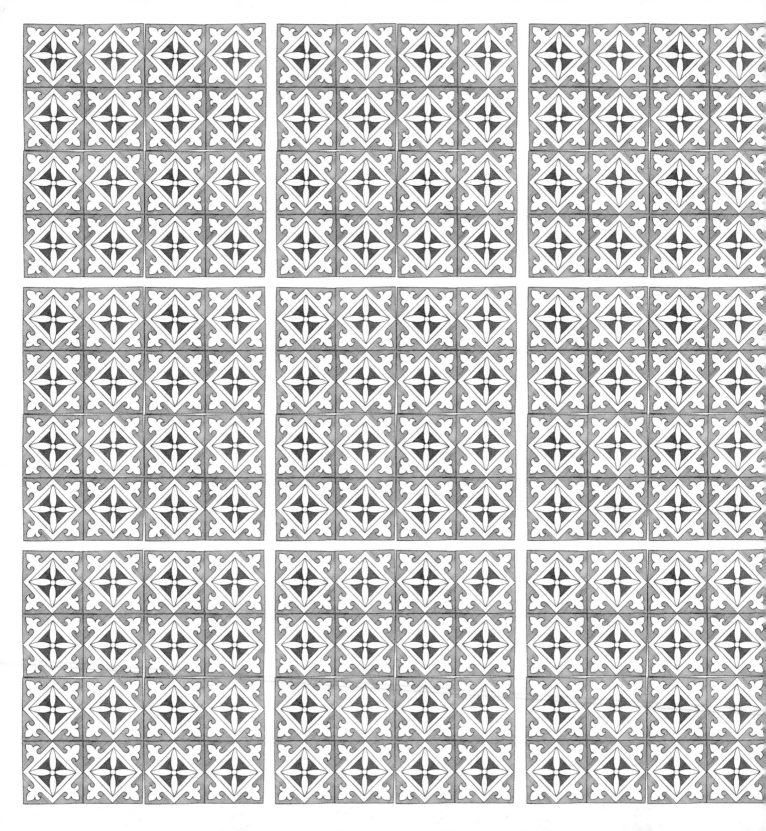